THE 13 NiGHTS OF HALLOWeeN

By Guy Vasilovich

HARPER
An Imprint of HarperCollinsPublishers

To wifey, Linda—for all her support
—G.V.

The 13 Nights of Halloween

Copyright © 2011 by Guy Vasilovich

All rights reserved. Manufactured in China.

No part of this book may be used or reproduced in any manner whatsoever
without written permission except in the case of brief quotations embodied
in critical articles and reviews. For information address HarperCollins
Children's Books, a division of HarperCollins Publishers, 10 East 53rd Street,
New York, NY 10022.

www.harpercollinschildrens.com

Library of Congress Cataloging-in-Publication Data

Vasilovich, Guy.

    The 13 nights of Halloween / by Guy Vasilovich.

        p.   cm.

    Summary: A Halloween version of "The Twelve Days of Christmas,"
featuring macabre gifts such as icky eyeballs, demons dancing, and thirsty
vampires.

    ISBN 978-0-06-180445-8 (trade bdg.)

    ISBN 978-0-06-180446-5 (lib. bdg.)

    1. Children's songs—United States—Texts.   [1. Halloween—Songs and
music.   2. Songs.]   I. Title.   II. Title: Thirteen nights of Halloween.

PZ8.3.V7125342Thi   2011   2009029469

782.421—dc22

[[E]]

Typography by Jeanne L. Hogle

11 12 13 14 15   SCP   10 9 8 7 6 5 4 3 2 1

❖

First Edition

On the first night of Halloween
my mummy gave to me:
a bright,
shiny

Skeleton Key

On the second night
of Halloween my
mummy gave to me:
a 2-headed Snake
and a
bright,
shiny
Skeleton Key

On the third night of Halloween
my mummy gave to me:

3 Baseball Bats

a 2-headed Snake,

and a

bright,

shiny

Skeleton Key

On the fourth night of
Halloween my mummy
gave to me:

4 Icky Eyeballs

3 Baseball Bats,

a 2-headed Snake,

and a

bright,

shiny

Skeleton Key

On the fifth night of Halloween
my mummy gave to me:

5 Singing Skulls

4 Icky Eyeballs,

3 Baseball Bats,

a *2*-headed Snake,

and a

bright,

shiny

Skeleton Key

On the sixth night of Halloween
my mummy gave to me:

6 Corpses Caroling

5 Singing Skulls,

4 Icky Eyeballs,

3 Baseball Bats,

a 2-headed Snake,

and a

bright,

shiny

Skeleton Key

On the seventh night
of Halloween my
mummy gave to me:

7 Goblins Gobbling

6 Corpses Caroling,

5 Singing Skulls,

4 Icky Eyeballs,

3 Baseball Bats,

a 2-headed Snake,

and a

bright,

shiny

Skeleton Key

On the eighth night of
Halloween my mummy
gave to me:
8 Marching Mutants

7 Goblins Gobbling,

6 Corpses Caroling,

5 Singing Skulls,

4 Icky Eyeballs,

3 Baseball Bats,

a 2 -headed Snake,

and a

a bright,

shiny

Skeleton Key

On the ninth night of Halloween
my mummy gave to me:

9 Werewolves Waiting,

8 Marching Mutants,

7 Goblins Gobbling,

6 Corpses Caroling,

5 Singing Skulls,

4 Icky Eyeballs,

Baseball Bats, a 2-headed Snake,

and a bright, shiny

Skeleton Key

On the tenth night
of Halloween my
mummy gave to me:
10 Demons Dancing

9 Werewolves Waiting,
8 Marching Mutants, 7 Goblins Gobbling,
6 Corpses Caroling, 5 Singing Skulls,
4 Icky Eyeballs, 3 Baseball Bats,
a 2-headed Snake,
and a
bright,
shiny
Skeleton Key

On the eleventh night of Halloween
my mummy gave to me:
11 Witches Witching

10 Demons Dancing,

9 Werewolves Waiting,

8 Marching Mutants,

7 Goblins Gobbling,

6 Corpses Caroling,

5 Singing Skulls,

4 Icky Eyeballs,

3 Baseball Bats,

a 2-headed Snake,

and a

bright,

shiny

Skeleton Key

On the twelfth night of Halloween my mummy gave to me:

12 Ghosts a-Ghosting

11 Witches Witching, 10 Demons Dancing, 9 Werewolves Waiting, 8 Marching Mutants, 7 Goblins Gobbling, 6 Corpses Caroling, 5 Singing Skulls, 4 Icky Eyeballs, 3 Baseball Bats, a 2 -headed Snake,

and a

bright,

shiny

Skeleton Key

On the thirteenth night
of Halloween
my mummy
gave to me:

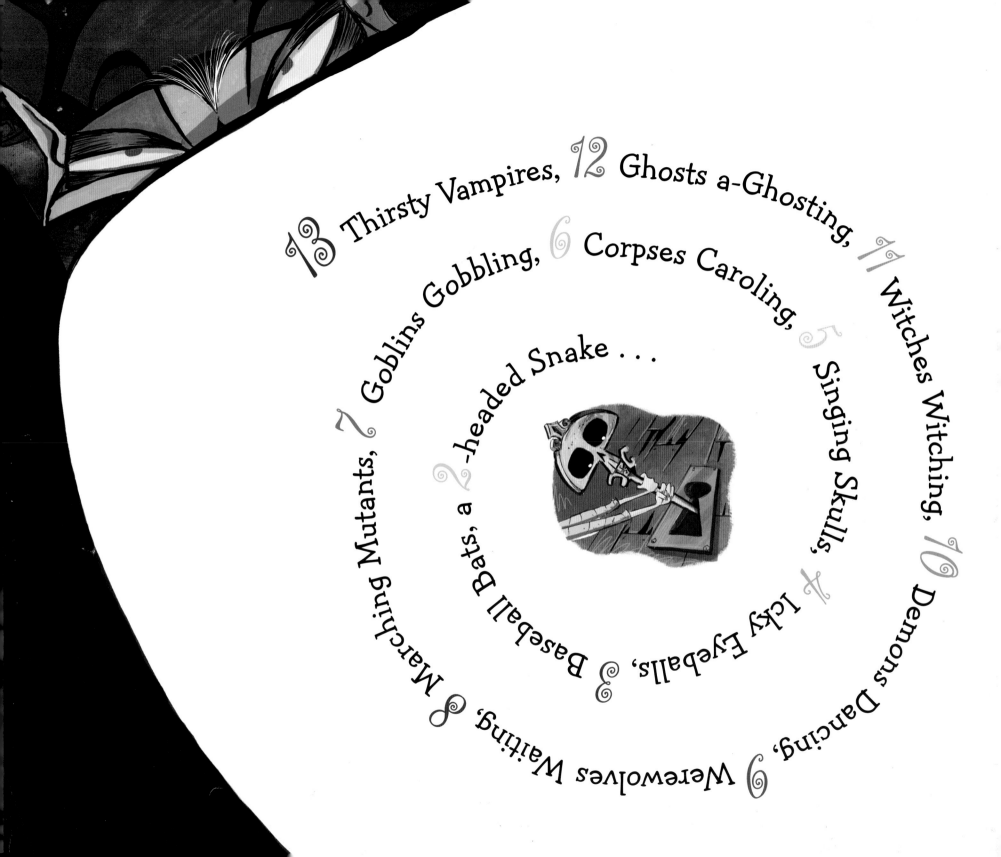

13 Thirsty Vampires, 12 Ghosts a-Ghosting, 11 Witches Witching, 10 Demons Dancing, 9 Werewolves Waiting, 8 Marching Mutants, 7 Goblins Gobbling, 6 Corpses Caroling, 5 Singing Skulls, 4 Icky Eyeballs, 3 Baseball Bats, a 2-headed Snake . . .

and a bright, shiny

Skeleton Key